To Sergey

STERLING CHILDREN'S BOOKS
New York

An Imprint of Sterling Publishing
1166 Avenue of the Americas
New York NY 10036

First Sterling edition published in 2015.

Originally published in 2013 in the United Kingdom by
Macmillan Children's Books,
a division of Macmillan Publishers Limited
20 New Wharf Road, London N1 9RR
Basingstoke and Oxford Associates companies throughout the world

Text and Illustrations © 2013 by Ekaterina Trukhan

ISBN 978-1-4549-1613-0

Distributed in Canada by Sterling Publishing
c/o Canadian Manda Group, 664 Annette Street
Toronto, Ontario, Canada M6S 2C8

For information about custom editions, special sales, and premium and corporate purchases,
please contact Sterling Special Sales at 800-805-5489 or specialsales@sterlingpublishing.com.

Printed in China

Lot #:
2 4 6 8 10 9 7 5 3 1
05/15

www.sterlingpublishing.com/kids

Ekaterina Trukhan

PATRICK
WANTS A
DOG!

STERLING CHILDREN'S BOOKS

New York

Patrick wanted a dog.

He dreamed of long walks
in the park and big
doggy cuddles.

But when he asked his parents, sometimes they didn't hear him,

sometimes they were too busy,

and sometimes they said "maybe."

But they never said "yes."

So Patrick decided that if they
wouldn't get him a dog . . .

he'd go out and find one himself.

He gathered together all the things he'd need,

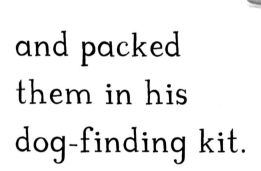

and packed them in his dog-finding kit.

He put on his favorite sweater . . .

and then he was off on his adventure!

WOOF
WOOF

GRRRR

First Patrick looked
in the park.

But all the dogs
there had owners.

So he went to the playground.
Patrick searched high . . .

and low.

But he didn't
find any dogs.

Next he tried
the pet shop.

There were
lots of
animals . . .

2 FOR 1

but not one single dog!

Then suddenly Patrick saw a tail!

But he wasn't interested in cats.
And they weren't interested in him.

Patrick was fed up.
Patrick was hungry.
Patrick wanted to go home.

He walked up
and down,
and round
and round . . .

but he was lost!

First Patrick couldn't find a dog,
now he couldn't find his way home.

And just when he thought that things couldn't get any worse . . .

a shadow crept slowly up the wall.
It was . . .

A MONSTER!

Patrick ran as fast as he could.
But the monster followed him!

It was so fast!
They ran until Patrick couldn't run anymore.

He could feel the monster's
warm breath getting closer.

It opened its mouth wide . . .

. . . and gave Patrick a big, sloppy lick.

Patrick was so relieved! He wasn't going to be eaten, and he'd found his way home.

But best of all . . .

... he got what he'd always wanted.

And Monster
got a home, too.